grade

5

GW00401780

For full details of exam requirements, please refer to the current syllabus in conjunction with *Examination Information & Regulations* and the guide for candidates, teachers and parents, *These Music Exams*. These three documents are available online at www.abrsm.org, as well as free of charge from music retailers, from ABRSM local representatives or from the Services Department, The Associated Board of the Royal Schools of Music, 24 Portland Place, London W1B 1LU, United Kingdom.

CONTENTS AND TRACK LISTING

Clarinet & Piano / *Piano only*

In this album, editorial additions to the texts are given in small print, within square brackets, or – in the case of slurs and ties – in the form ⌒ . Metronome marks, breath marks (retained here where they appear in the source edition) and ornament realizations (suggested for exam purposes) are for guidance only; they are not comprehensive or obligatory.

Footnotes: Anthony Burton

Alternative pieces for this grade

Music origination by Barnes Music Engraving Ltd
Cover by Økvik Design
Printed in England by Halstan and Co. Ltd, Amersham, Bucks.

21.00

Tarantella

No. 41 from *Vollständige Clarinett-Schule*, Op. 63

A:1

Arranged by
Paul Harris and Emma Johnson

C. BAERMANN

Carl Baermann (1811–85) was the son of the great clarinettist Heinrich Baermann, for whom Weber wrote most of his clarinet music. As a young man, Carl travelled with his father on concert tours; Mendelssohn wrote his two Concert Pieces for them – Heinrich on clarinet and Carl on basset-horn. Carl later succeeded his father as principal clarinettist of the Munich court orchestra. He was also a prolific composer, the inventor of an improved 18-keyed clarinet, and the author of a widely used *Complete Method for Clarinet*, which appeared in instalments between 1864 and 1875. This tutor is the source of his *Tarantella*, reproduced here in a slightly shortened version. A tarantella is a dance in fast compound time or triplets, originally from the southern Italian town of Taranto, where it was popularly supposed to be a cure for the bite of the local tarantula spider.

A:2

Frühlingslied

No. 6 from *Lieder ohne Worte*, Op. 62

Arranged by
Thea King and Alan Frank

MENDELSSOHN

Frühlingslied Spring Song;   **Lieder ohne Worte** Songs without Words

Felix Mendelssohn (1809–47) composed eight books of *Songs without Words* for piano, six pieces in each, between about 1829 and 1845; they became very popular with domestic pianists both in his native Germany and in Victorian England. Ten of these pieces were freely adapted by the clarinettist Dame Thea King and the publisher and composer Alan Frank for an album called *Mendelssohn for the Clarinet*. This is one of the best known of the whole series, composed in 1842 and published in 1844 as the last piece in Book Six; it was given the title 'Spring Song' by a friend of the composer. Notice that the melody does not fall into quite such regular four-bar phrases as you might expect!

© 1993 by The Associated Board of the Royal Schools of Music
Reproduced from *Mendelssohn for the Clarinet* arranged by Thea King and Alan Frank (ABRSM Publishing)

Allegro moderato

First movement from Sonata No. 3 in F

Edited by
John Davies and Paul Harris

Keyboard realization by
David Rowland

LEFÈVRE

Xavier Lefèvre (1763–1829) was a Swiss-born clarinettist who established himself in Paris as a performer and composer for his instrument. He taught at the Paris Conservatoire from its foundation in 1795 until 1824, and in 1802 published his *Méthode de clarinette*, which was adopted by the Conservatoire and many other teaching institutions. This method ends with 12 sonatas for clarinet with a bass line – probably the basis for an old-fashioned keyboard continuo accompaniment, though it could be played just on a cello or bassoon. The first movement of Sonata No. 3 is given here with an editorial keyboard realization, and suggestions for additional phrasing and dynamics. The editors also draw attention to the two different staccato signs that appear in the original; on the basis of Lefèvre's introduction to his *Méthode*, they suggest that notes with dots 'should be lightly articulated and played for about half their written duration', while those with wedges [ᵛ] 'are to be more markedly detached with some degree of accentuation'.

© Oxford University Press 1988

Reproduced from Lefèvre: *Five Sonatas for Clarinet* by permission. All enquiries about this piece, apart from those directly relating to the exams, should be addressed to Oxford University Press, Music Department, Great Clarendon Street, Oxford OX2 6DP.

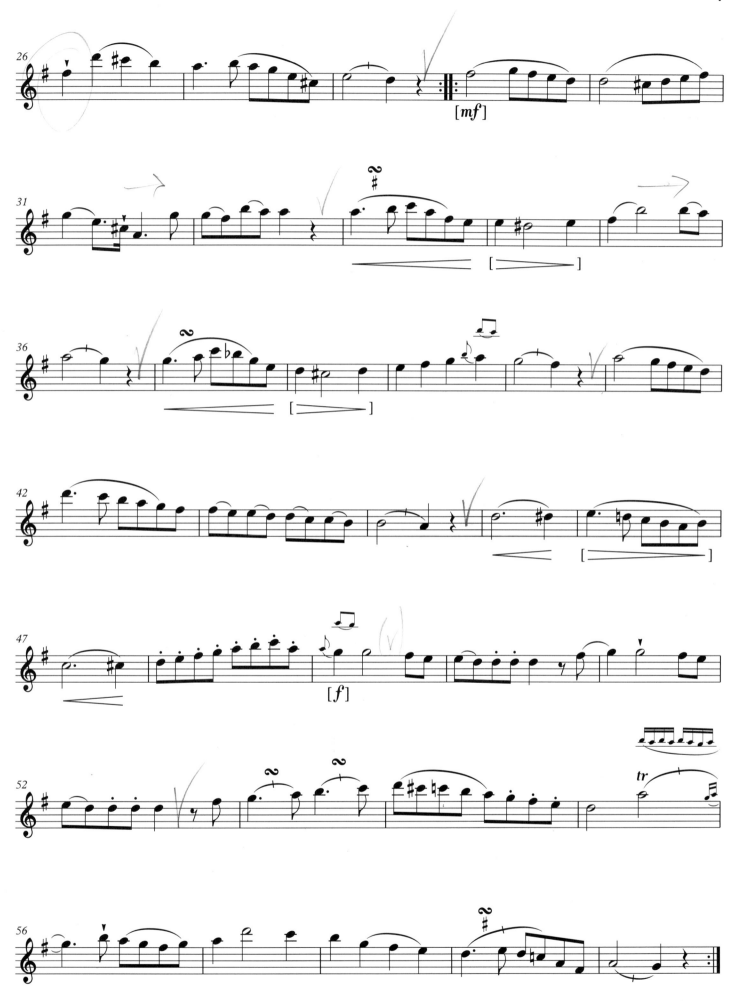

B:1

Burlesque

No. 4 from *Four Short Pieces*, Op. 6

FERGUSON

Belfast-born, Howard Ferguson (1908–99) was a rare example of a composer who retired: after writing fewer than two dozen works, culminating in the late 1950s in two large-scale cantatas for chorus and orchestra, he decided (in the words of Michael Hurd) 'that he had said all he wished to say as a composer and courageously determined to write no more' (*The New Grove Dictionary of Music and Musicians* (London, 2001)). He was also active as a pianist, a teacher at the Royal Academy of Music in London, and an editor of early keyboard music. 'Burlesque' – the title implies a light, humorous composition – is the last of a set of *Four Short Pieces* for clarinet or viola and piano, which Ferguson composed between 1932 and 1936. An acceptable tempo for this piece in the exam would be ♩ = *c*.72.

B:2

Frensham Pond

Aquarelle for Clarinet and Piano
from *Country Impressions*

W. LLOYD WEBBER

William Lloyd Webber (1914–82) was a professor at the Royal College of Music and later director of the London College of Music, an organist, and the composer of several large-scale sacred choral works and many shorter pieces. (He was also the father of two musically talented sons, Andrew and Julian, one the famous composer of musicals and the other the celebrated cellist.) This piece is one of a set of *Country Impressions* for various different wind instruments and piano, published in 1960. Frensham Pond is a well-known beauty spot in Surrey, south-west of London; an 'aquarelle', appropriately enough, is a type of painting in water-colour.

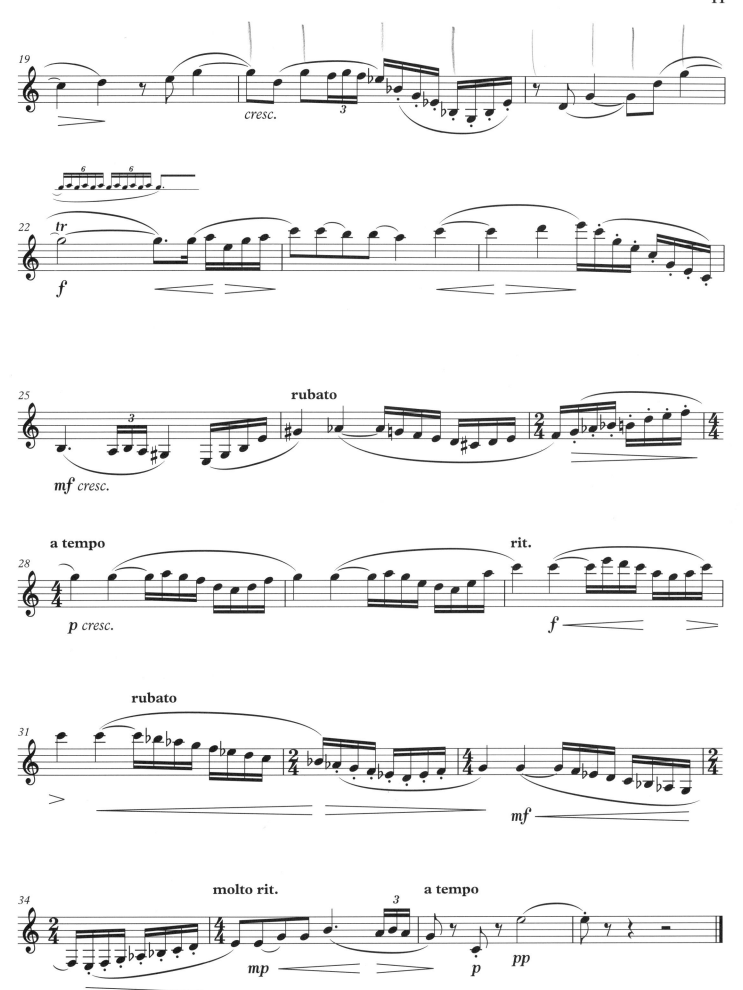

B:3

Turkey in the Straw

No. 1 from *The Christopher Norton Concert Collection for Clarinet*

CHRISTOPHER NORTON

Born in New Zealand in 1953, Christopher Norton is one of Britain's leading composers of educational music, well known for his *Microjazz* and *Microstyles* series and for his *Concert Collections* for piano, clarinet and flute. The first piece in the collection for clarinet is an exuberant treatment of *Turkey in the Straw*, an anonymous song made popular by American minstrels in the 1820s and 1830s, and now perhaps more familiar as a fiddle tune. In the exam, the notes in the final two bars may be played in either octave – but note the extreme dynamic marking!

Scaredy Cat

ROB BUCKLAND

Rob Buckland (b. 1967) is a well-known saxophonist, a member of the Apollo Saxophone Quartet and a soloist in both jazz and classical music. He is also professor of saxophone at the Royal Northern College of Music in Manchester, and a composer of concert and educational music. He describes this piece as 'a simple "swing" study', and suggests that to set the right mood you might 'imagine a cat walking in a "cool" way but occasionally being startled'.

AB 3351

Theme and Variation 14

from *Rhapsody on a Theme of Paganini*, Op. 43

Arranged by
Russell Denwood

RACHMANINOFF

There are three composers involved here. Nicolò Paganini (1782–1840) was a famous Italian violin virtuoso, whose works include a set of 24 Caprices for solo violin, published in 1820; the last of these consists of variations on a simple theme. This theme has subsequently been used for sets of variations by many other composers, from Brahms to Andrew Lloyd Webber. Among them was the great Russian-born pianist, conductor and composer Serge Rachmaninoff (1873–1943), with his *Rhapsody on a Theme of Paganini* for piano and orchestra, written and first performed in 1934. And that brings us to Russell Denwood (b. 1950), a former bassoonist and woodwind teacher in the north of England, who had the idea of adapting Paganini's theme and some of Rachmaninoff's variations as studies of varying difficulty for solo clarinet. In the exam, the repeats should be observed.

Study in D minor

from *Praktische Stakkato-Schule für Klarinette*, Op. 53

C:3

Edited by
John Davies and Paul Harris

STARK

The German clarinettist Robert Stark (1847–1922) played in the orchestras of Chemnitz and Wiesbaden, but then spent the rest of his career as a teacher at the Würzburg School of Music. He published concertos and other pieces for his instrument, an important tutor for clarinet, basset-horn and bass clarinet, and some other teaching works. This study in fast staccato with offbeat accents at varying dynamics is from his *Practical Staccato School*, published in 1909.

Reproduced from *80 Graded Studies for Clarinet*, Book 1, by permission of the publishers. All enquiries about this piece, apart from those directly relating to the exams, should be addressed to Faber Music Ltd, 3 Queen Square, London WC1N 3AU.

C MAJOR$^{(2)}$ — A NATURAL$^{(2)}$ — A HARMONIC$^{(2)}$ — A MELODIC$^{(2)}$ — G^7 — D^{-7}

F MAJOR$^{(2)}$ — D NATURAL$^{(2)}$ — D HARMONIC$^{(2)}$ — D MELODIC$^{(2)}$ — C^7 — G^{-7}

G MAJOR$^{(2)}$ — E NATURAL$^{(3)}$ — E HARMONIC$^{(3)}$ — E MELODIC$^{(3)}$ — D^7

Bb MAJOR$^{(2)}$ — G NATURAL$^{(2)}$ — G HARMONIC$^{(2)}$ — G MELODIC$^{(2)}$ — F^7

D MAJOR$^{(2)}$ — B NATURAL$^{(2)}$ — B HARMONIC$^{(2)}$ — B MELODIC$^{(2)}$ — A^7 — E^{-7}

Eb MAJOR$^{(2)}$ — C NATURAL$^{(2)}$ — C HARMONIC$^{(2)}$ — C MELODIC$^{(2)}$ — Bb^7 — F^{-7}

A MAJOR$^{-(2)}$ — F# NATURAL$^{(2)}$ — F# HARMONIC$^{(2)}$ — F# MELODIC$^{(2)}$ — E^7

Ab MAJOR$^{(2)}$ — F NATURAL$^{(2)}$ — F HARMONIC$^{(2)}$ — F MELODIC$^{(2)}$ — Eb^7

E MAJOR$^{(3)}$ — C# NATURAL$^{(2)}$ — C# HARMONIC$^{(2)}$ — C# MELODIC$^{(2)}$ — B^7

Db MAJOR$^{(2)}$ — Bb NATURAL — Bb HARMONIC — Bb MELODIC — Ab^7

B MAJOR$^{(2)}$ — G# NATURAL$^{(2)}$ — G# HARMONIC$^{(2)}$ — G# MELODIC$^{(2)}$ — F#^{7}

F# MAJOR$^{(2)}$ — D# NATURAL$^{(2)}$ — D# HARMONIC$^{(2)}$ — D# MELODIC$^{(2)}$ — C#^{7}

Gb MAJOR — Eb NATURAL — Eb HARMONIC — Eb MELODIC — Db^7

C# MAJOR — A# NATURAL — A# HARMONIC — A# MELODIC — G#^{7}

Cb MAJOR — Ab NATURAL — Ab HARMONIC — Ab MELODIC — Gb$^>$

DOMINANT IN THE KEY of : G$^{(2)}$, C$^{(2)}$, Bb$^{(2)}$, D$^{(2)}$, A$^{(3)}$

DIMINISHED 7TH on : G$^{(2)}$, E$^{(3)}$, C$^{(2)}$

CHROMATIC on G$^{(2)}$, F$^{(2)}$, C$^{(2)}$, A$^{(2)}$, E$^{(3)}$